KID GUARDIANS®

Planet Earth Patrol

SERIES ™

# What Is Global Warming?

by
Richard D. Covey
& Diane H. Pappas

Illustrated by
The Pixel Factory

D1416123

SCHOLASTIC INC.
New York  Toronto  London  Auckland  Sydney
Mexico City  New Delhi  Hong Kong  Buenos Aires

To Nikos, we hope some day you may help solve the problem.
Love, R.D.C. and D.H.P.

Special thanks to the talented artists of The Pixel Factory,
Willie Castro, Desma Thompson, & Bob Duane

————————————————

ISBN-13: 978-0-545-06104-9
ISBN-10: 0-545-06104-0

Text and illustrations copyright © 2009 by A G Education, Inc.

12 11 10 9 8 7 6 5 4 3 2 1    9 10 11 12 13 14/0

Printed in the U.S.A.
First printing, March 2009

## MEET THE KID GUARDIANS

From their home base in the mystical Himalayan mountain kingdom of Shambala, Zak the Yak and the Kid Guardians are always on alert, ready to protect the children of the world from danger.

**ZAK THE YAK** is a gentle giant with a heart of gold. He's the leader of the Kid Guardians.

Loyal and lovable, **SCRUBBER** is Zak's best friend and sidekick.

**BUZZER** is both street-smart and book-smart, with a real soft spot for kids.

Always curious about the world, **SMOOCH** loves to meet new people and see new places.

**CARROT**, with her wild red hair, is funny, lovable, and the first to jump in when help is needed.

Whenever a child is in danger, the **TROUBLE BUBBLE**™ sounds an alarm and then instantly transports the Kid Guardians to that location.

"Welcome to the United Nations," said Dr. Rhandi. "Today we're going to learn about the problem of global warming. Scientists believe that the air in our atmosphere is holding in more heat than it used to."

Global warming has increased world temperatures. The warmer air melts glaciers, raises sea levels, and changes climates all round the world."

"Come on, Carrot, let's go!" Zak said. "We're going to help our friend, Dr. Rhandi, talk to the kids about global warming."

Hi, Dr. Rhandi! Hi, kids! I'm Zak the Yak, leader of the Kid
Guardians, and this is Carrot. We'll help explain why both humans
and nature cause global warming and why it's a problem. Then
we can all work together to start fixing it."

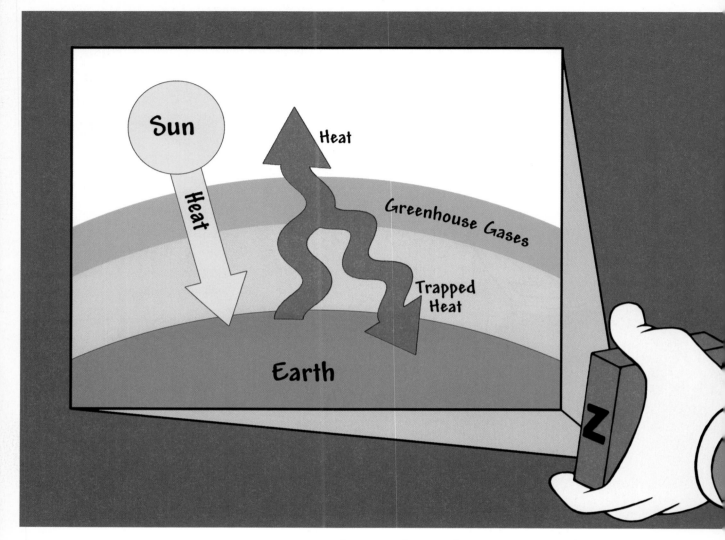

"Warm air rises, carrying carbon dioxide created from car exhaust and smoke from factories. These greenhouse gases act like glass windows in the sky. They trap the heat in the atmosphere. This is called the 'Greenhouse Effect.'"

Look at these polar bears," explained Carrot. "Now they must swim farther to find food. Glaciers and ice packs are melting faster than they can be created. Seals rest on the ice. With less ice, there are fewer seals, which means less food for the polar bears."

"The water from the melted glaciers makes the sea level rise," explained Zak. "When the ocean level gets too high, villages and houses on some islands will flood. The villagers will have to leave."

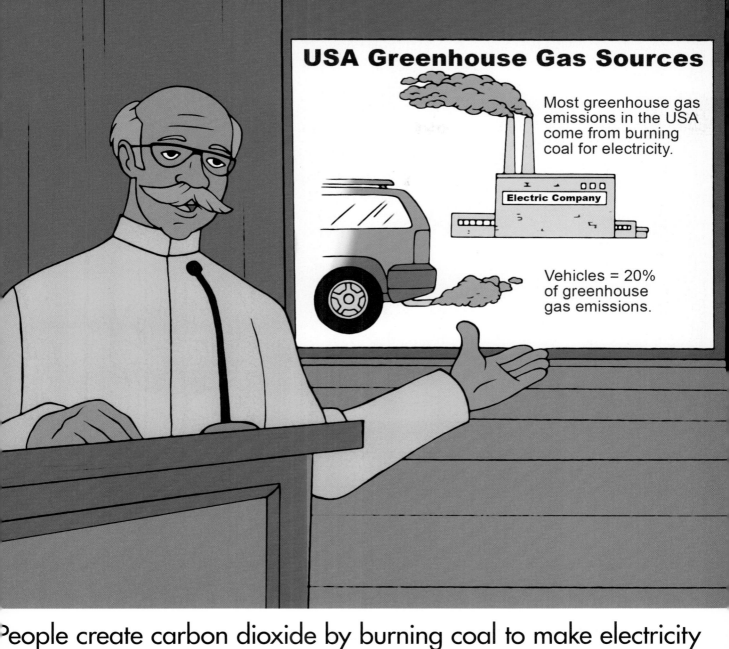

"People create carbon dioxide by burning coal to make electricity and by driving cars. Scientists are now working on ways to reduce carbon dioxide emissions," said Dr. Rhandi.

"Some scientists think volcanoes and other natural causes are the main source of global warming," Zak said.

"Although we can't change natural events like volcanoes," said Carrot, "I know what we can do! Let's plant trees!"

Back at school the next day...

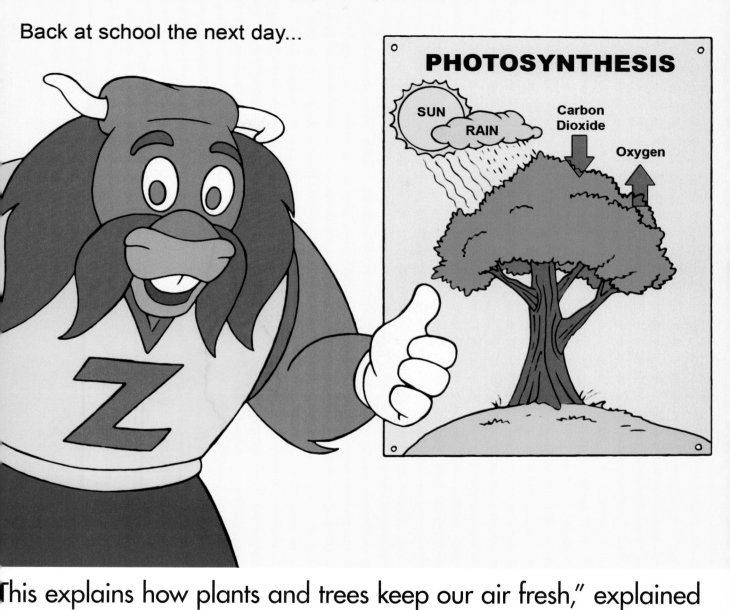

"This explains how plants and trees keep our air fresh," explained
ak. "Trees take in sunlight, carbon dioxide, and water to make
od. They release fresh oxygen into the air. Trees are good for
e planet and help reduce carbon dioxide in the air."

At a park several weekends later . . .

"Kids, I am so proud you are planting all these trees," said Carro
"Because of your hard work, the air will be better for the future.
As these trees grow, they will make the air much cleaner and
fresher for everybody."

We should try to suggest ways to plant more trees to our friends and families," said Zak. "You could plant a tree to honor your family or for a friend's birthday. Some people plant as many trees as were needed to build their house."

"Kids, here are some ways you can help reduce global warming," said Zak.

1. Start a recycling program.
2. Walk or ride your bicycle when you can.
3. Keep planting trees.